From Me

to You

For Catherine, Alastair
Sam and Olly
and for Martine

All my love ... AF

Text copyright © 2003 by Anthony France
Illustrations copyright © 2003 by Tiphanie Beeke

First U.S. edition 2004

Library of Congress Cataloging-in-Publication Data is available.
Library of Congress Catalog Card Number 2002041574
ISBN 0-7636-2255-9

First published in 2003 by Gullane Children's Books Limited,
Winchester House, 259-269 Old Marylebone Road, London NW1 5XJ

2 4 6 8 10 9 7 5 3 1

Printed in China

This book was typeset in Mrs Eaves Roman.
The illustrations were done in watercolor.

Candlewick Press
2067 Massachusetts Avenue
Cambridge, Massachusetts 02140

visit us at www.candlewick.com

for my little friend
Daniel J
with love TB.

From Me to You

Anthony France illustrated by **Tiphanie Beeke**

CANDLEWICK PRESS
CAMBRIDGE, MASSACHUSETTS

A happy morning was struggling to find its way into Rat's bedroom, but Rat was feeling miserable. Not wanting to get up and not wanting to stay in bed, he knew he was in for another case of the bathrobe blues.

The bathrobe blues are when you don't
wash your face or comb your whiskers and just
mope around all day long in your bathrobe. Rat was
good at this. He did it every day.

Wearing his bathrobe, Rat slunk downstairs.

For breakfast, Rat had a stale muffin and a cold cup of yesterday's leftover tea.

"I don't have anything to do," he thought, "and I don't have anyone to do it with. My friends never come to see me these days, and doing nothing with no one is no fun at all."

Rat was sighing a very sad sigh indeed, when he heard his mailbox clank. Curious, he went to look and discovered a cheerful yellow envelope.

Rat opened it and read:

Dear Rat,
This letter is from someone who really admires you. I think you are very special, and I just want you to know how lucky I feel to have such a true and dear friend as you.

All my love...

But there was no name at the bottom.

Rat read the letter again. And then, just to make sure, he read it another ten times.

"How wonderful!" said Rat. "But I have no idea who sent it . . . unless . . . why, of course, it must be from Mouse! How very kind of him. I'll go and thank him right away."

He shot upstairs,
yanked off his bathrobe,

pulled on some clothes,

washed his face,

brushed his teeth,   combed his whiskers,

and skipped out into the morning, clutching his letter.

Mouse was delighted to see Rat. "It's a lovely letter," said Mouse, "but since the storm, I haven't written to anyone. I've been busy repairing my roof."

Rat was sorry to learn about Mouse's damaged roof, and for the rest of the day they worked together to fix it.

When they had finished and were having some tea, Mouse
wondered aloud, "Who *do* you think sent that letter?"

"Beats me," said Rat, who felt happy just thinking about it.
"But I'll find out tomorrow."

The next morning, Rat washed, dressed, and was downstairs before dawn. He made a fresh pot of tea and a fresh batch of muffins.

Rat was now almost certain that the someone who loved him was Frog. She hadn't been to see him for ages, so he would go and see her. He stepped out of his house just as the sun was rising over the fields.

Rat knocked at Frog's door for a long time
before he heard a faint voice from inside.
"Who is it?" asked Frog.

"It's me," said Rat. "Is anything wrong?"

"Nothing much," replied Frog, "but you'll
have to let yourself in."

Rat was shocked to discover that Frog had broken her leg.

"I'm all right," said Frog. "It's been a bit difficult, just hopping around in circles, but lots of friends have dropped by to help."

"I'd have dropped by, too, if I'd known," said Rat, guiltily chewing a whisker. "So, can I help you now?" he asked.

It was not until Rat was out shopping for Frog that he realized he had forgotten to ask about the letter.

He compared Frog's handwritten shopping list . . .

TOMATOES
LEEKS
RADISHES
PACKET
OF OATMEAL

Rat
Flowerpot House

to the words on his yellow envelope . . .

and he knew one thing for sure. The letter had not been written by Frog.

"Wake up, daydreamer," a voice said suddenly. "What have you got that's so interesting?" asked another voice. It was Rat's friends Mr. and Mrs. Mole and their son, Baby Mole.

"Somebody sent me a letter," answered Rat, "but I don't know who."

"Well, it's not from us," said the Moles. "We haven't written, but we stopped by your house the other day."

"You did?" asked Rat.

"On Wednesday afternoon," said Mrs. Mole. "Your curtains were closed, so we left you in peace."

Rat finished the shopping and returned to Frog's house. He had planned to make her lunch, but Mouse had turned up with a pie.

"Any luck with your mysterious letter writer?" asked Mouse.

Rat shook his head. But then, for the briefest of moments, he thought he saw Mouse wink at Frog.

After lunch, Rat set off once again to solve the mystery. He felt on top of the world. He had spent so much time wondering who thought he was special that he actually was beginning to feel special.

He now decided to pay Bat a visit.

Rat knocked on Bat's door.

"Who's that?" said Bat. "What do you want?"

"It's Rat, Bat," said Rat. "Hello!"

"Goodbye," said Bat. "I'm busy!"

"But it's me, your friend," pleaded Rat. "I want to know how you are . . . and whether you've written to me recently."

"Of course not," said Bat. "Nobody writes to me, so I don't write to anybody. And if you were a real friend, you'd have come over before now. So goodbye."

Something was obviously wrong with Bat. He was lonely and unhappy—and what's more, he was still in his bathrobe.

It was a sorry Rat who got home that evening—only he was no longer sorry for himself.

"Poor old Bat," he whispered. "He's down in the dumps, but what he said is right. If I were a real friend, I would have visited him before. The only reason I went today was to find out something for myself."

And then Rat read his precious letter for the last time. "Finding out who wrote this just doesn't seem important anymore," he thought. "I don't deserve it, no matter who sent it. I've never been a true friend to anyone."

"Tomorrow," said Rat, "I'm going to change all that."

Rat had gone to bed with the seed of an idea, but it soon grew into an entire plan. Rat got up at six to get started.

He woke up Mouse first.

"I've written lots of invitations for a party, and I want you and Frog to help me deliver them. What do you think of that?"

At six in the morning, Mouse seldom thought much about anything, but by seven, he was more excited than Rat.

"Let's get Frog," he said.

The three of them had great fun that day. Mouse was glad to leave his roof, Frog enjoyed the fresh air, and Rat just liked being with his friends. They walked for miles, and by late afternoon, all the invitations were delivered.

All except one.

Bat's curtains were still closed
when they arrived at his house.
Rat quietly pushed the invitation
into the mailbox. Then he pulled
a bright red envelope from his
pocket and slid that in, too.

"What's that?" asked Mouse.
"Just a special letter for Bat,"
whispered Rat. "That's all."
And then, for the briefest of
moments, Mouse and Frog
thought Rat winked at them—
and they were right. He did.